DARKNESS 102

Advanced Lessons Were Learned

ELIZABETH SUGGS   JONATHAN REDDOCH

MICHAELA RAE   ALEX CHILD   JENNIFER LEO

NATALYA MONYOK   STEVE CAPONE JR.

H. V. PATTERSON   JORDAN MCCLYMONT

ERIC J. GUIGNARD   ASHLEY HUYGE   F. MALANOCHE

PUCK PHILLIPS   ROBIN KNABEL   TYLER J. WELCH

JESSICA GLEASON   KELLI DIANNE RULE

MORGANA PRICE   K. R. PATTERSON

CAILÍN FRANKLAND   BRIANNA MALOTKE

AUDRAKATE GONZALEZ   CHRIS JORGENSEN

JOSHUA BOOKER   SARA FITZGERALD

HANNAH GRACE   CHARLES KYD   ANNE GREGG

PETER L. HARMON   ROBERT J. FOSTER

THOMAS S. SALEM   ETHAN STEWART

JENNY CASTRO   ACE MACK   JESSICA GLEASON

ANDREW J. PIXTON   DEBRA BIRDWELL WINKLER

PAUL LONARDO   DEVIN GUIGNARD   MAE THORN

JO BIRDWELL   MAKAYLA NIELSON

SELENE IBARRA RUBIO   P. S. TOM   J. B. CORSO

JAYNE ANN OSBORNE   JACEK WILKOS   M. L. SMYTHE

CORINNE POLLARD   ELIZABETH RAYNE

KEYRA K. ALLRED   GREGORY MEECE

RUSSELL EVANS   ADDISON HOPE

MADISON PARKER   AMBER BUCKLEY

Contents

Introduction

In 2023, *Darkness 101: Lessons Were Learned* featured the novel concept of publishing 101 stories, each 101 words. We had so much fun and such a positive response that we decided to do a follow-up with the "clever" concept of 102 stories all 102 words; thus, the book *Darkness 102: Advanced Lessons Were Learned* was born.

Many of our favorites returned like Alex Child, K. R. Patterson, Morgana Price, and AudraKate Gonzalez. We also have some new names joining us like Stoker-award-winning author Eric J. Guignard and honorary IronPen winner Michaela Rae.

We hope you enjoy our little "textbook," or at least learn something!

1

Body Count

Jonathan Reddoch

"Nine?" Bobby questioned his long-suffering fiancé. "Nine? Are you serious?"

"Yeah, it's not that high," Michelle said.

"I can't marry a girl with a body count that high."

"Why not?"

"It's just gross you know."

"It's not *that* gross! I have an industrial carpet cleaner."

"That's so disgusting." He shrunk into the couch with his head in his hands.

"I hate for it to end this way."

"Really, nine?"

She struck an ax into his spine. "Make that ten."

The blood had splattered across her new white blouse. "Ew," she mused, withdrawing the weapon from his back, "it is a little gross."

Rain Dance

Jennifer Leo

IN THE BLAZING SUN, Professor Smith examined trinkets unearthed from the red rock: pottery shards, a bone-bead necklace, a tattered moccasin. But the real treasure was a ceremonial gourd rattle—fully intact.

Smirking, he shook the rattle mocking a medicine dance in the dust. "Hi-ya-ya-yawh! Hi-ya-ya-yawh!"

A raindrop hit him in the eye. Then another pelted his cheek, followed by sheets of water drenching his clothes. Hurrying towards his Jeep, he slipped in a ditch. With a twisted ankle, he groaned as a torrent flooded down the channel, sweeping him into the current.

Minutes later, golden sun again filled the silent valley.

The Cave of Echoes

Michaela Rae

STELLA'S SECOND-GRADE class stumbled through the narrow tunnels of the Cave of Echoes, their yellow lights bouncing off stalagmites.

"Stay with your buddy, please!" Ms. Hannae instructed, counting twelve heads. Hazel squeezed Stella's hand.

"We're about to enter the *dark zone*—the most intense darkness you will ever experience," she said. "Okay, children! Turn off your lanterns in three… two… one!"

As long shadows engulfed them, silence swallowed their glee. The only sound was Stella's playful giggles.

When Ms. Hannae flipped the lights on, eleven tiny petrified faces stared at Hazel's empty palm.

All that remained of Stella was her lingering laughter.

The Man Inside Is Dangeours

Elizabeth Suggs

THE MAN INSIDE Is Dangeours

I stared at my computer. I'd pasted my story into the document, but it was gone. Just that phrase. Taunting me.

And they couldn't even spell.

Inside what? My computer? My house? I lived alone. I hadn't seen anyone in days—except the amateur plumber. But he'd left after I yelled at him.

Hadn't he?

From the screen's reflection, a shadow shifted behind me.

Panic rooted me in place.

The last thing I saw was the plumber raising a rusted wrench.

As it came down, I realized the warning wasn't a joke.

Just a little too late.

Shoplifters Will Not Be Prosecuted

H.V. Patterson

THE MANAGER SHOVED Amy into a dingy office and locked the door behind them.

"Hey! You can't keep me here!" she cried. "That's illegal!"

"You shoplifted," said the manager.

"Just lipstick!"

"*Just* lipstick—this time," the manager said. "And before that—*just* a hairbrush. And before that—*just* a pack of cigarettes. Shall I continue?"

"Are you going to call the police?" Amy asked, stomach sinking.

"No," said the manager. "That's not our policy."

He tapped a faded sign on the wall that read:

Shoplifters Will Be Devoured

The soundproofed office swallowed Amy's screams. The manager meticulously lapped up her splattered blood.

Selfie

Steve Capone Jr.

"Wouldn't do that if I were you," the know-it-all calls.

I inch forward, camera in hand.

Just a little bit closer.

The moose is huge. It lifts its horselike head. It regards me as it chews.

"Nice moose," I say. "There, there. Just a quick photo."

I turn and position the selfie stick.

"That's a wild animal!" another inbred local shouts at me.

I know a gentle giant when I see one.

A few steps more. I turn, holding up the phone and edging backward.

The beast grunts. I hear it shift.

I hear the warning: "No!"

A train hits me. Darkness.

The Mailbox on Mordoc Lane

Eric J. Guignard

AT THE OLD turnoff for Mordoc Lane, where the fire road cuts through, is a row of bungalows, stone constructs framed in peeling lattice—all since abandoned—wrapping around the scars of the mineworks.

Legend goes, a postman was delivering to the last house there, his hand inside the metal mailbox, when a flash of lightning struck, frying him to ash.

On full moons now, you might see that mailbox still, its little hinged door hung open, the postman's final delivery inside, glowing gold as dreams.

But if you should take what's inside, it's said the mailbox will take what's inside you.

Corpse Garden

Natalya Monyok

Virgil wheeled out Eliza's corpse, ripped through her plump chest, consumed her heart, and licked up the spilled blood with rapture.

He was looking at his lovely corpse garden, the endless steel drawers housing bodies ripe for the picking, when a fire raged through him and constricted his airway. He clawed at his throat and tried to crawl to the metal door, but then his body seized up, paralyzed.

At the height of his agony, a blurred figure loomed above him, but he received no response to his pathetic plea.

As darkness descended, the last thing he heard was, "The poison worked."

Hell of Hangover

Jonathan Reddoch

TRINA CREPT up to her dad's recliner, reaching for the shiny can of cheap light beer.

"No, you can't have that!" he muttered.

"Why not?" she said, looking down at her curled toes.

"It's bad for you."

"How come?"

"Causes brain damage." He took a sour gulp.

"It hurts your brains?"

"Yeah, that's why they call it *get'n hammered.*"

"Getting hammered feels good?"

"Sadly, yes." He put down his can. "Now say *goodnight* and go to bed."

Trina said *goodnight* and went into her little brother's room. She raised a hammer taken from her father's toolbox.

"We're going to get so drunk!"

Epigraphs of the Sun

Jordan McClymont

"WE WERE NAIVE REALLY, to think we could control such magic. But we were all just excited to be channeling something that ancient, but we were insects, and she was a tsunami. Many were evaporated at that first gathering, and the second, well, we all know what happened."

– Audio Recordings of Dr. Charlotte Ellis, the day of her suicide.

"And I began to see, not a cat, but a lioness—colossal and uncaring. With paws to shake the earth and a roar that deafened us all. Then, white and blinding, the bombs struck her…"

– Source Unknown
Early Sightings of the Sun Goddess

Sticks and Stones

Ashley Huyge

"Daddy says they're just words," Hank sniffles to the school psychologist. He wiped his nose with his sleeve, his feet dangling from the chair.

"He says I'm stupid," he sobs. "He says, 'Sticks and stones may break my bones, but words will never hurt me.'"

Ms. Meyerson scribbles on a scratch of paper. "His name is *James?*"

Hank nods.

The bell rings and Hank scrambles, Pavlovian, to catch the bus.

Ms. Meyerson pulls a doll made of twigs, twine, and magic from her drawer, fastening the name to the effigy.

"Just words, huh?" she mutters, bending the tiny leg until it snaps.

The Egyptologist's Dream

F. Malanoche

LIGHT BOUNCED off shined sheets of metal, illuminating the chamber. Professor Clarice Dumas waited the majority of her career to determine the death of Pharaoh Yakareb. She tried to translate as the men on the expedition took crowbars to the sarcophagus. Their grunting slowed her efforts, but she persevered.

As the lid of the pharaoh's final resting place thudded on the ground, she deciphered the inscription. It read: *the dark breath*. A cool gust ran through the chamber. Some diggers coughed. Others ran.

Clarice coughed into her handkerchief, horrified to see black mucus. Pharaoh Yakareb had the last laugh as she choked.

The Woods

Puck Phillips

THERE ARE some taboos so unspoken, and yet so plain to the elders, that the child cannot but see in their violation the fulfillment of a lost destiny. The child goes into the dark wood filled with oaks, so cavernous and stifling. He goes in and is swallowed by the nameless and ancient evil.

In his last moments alive, he sees what would have been his legacy had he not ventured into the woods. He sees a wife, a child, and he tells the child everything his parents were scared of. He sees this vision of life devoured first—then, his legs.

Closer

Robin Knabel

"Don't sit close, James! It'll be the death of you."

"Thanks, Mom," I drone, flicking on the tube as she heads upstairs.

Elvira appears.

I inch closer, mesmerized.

As if sensing my presence, she stops and turns toward me.

"James," she purrs.

"Is this real?"

Before she answers, I lunge forward.

Pressing both palms against the convex glass, electricity crackles.

My hair stands on end.

"Kiss me," she says.

White-hot energy arcs, our lips fuse.

Her face melts, molten glass seals my mouth and eyes.

I hear the basement door.

"James! Turn that off! It'll be the death of you!"

She's right.

The District

Tyler J. Welch

ANOTHER FAMILIAR SCENE—HER arms are cut off, her legs are cut off, her head… cut off.

The flash of a colleague's camera strobes the room, though I don't blink, my eyes as focused as the pen across my pad of paper. Murmurs ricochet off the cauliflower-painted walls, smashing together, all incoherent bustling white noise to my distant ears.

This scene, much like those before, brings with it a pleasure. I'm lost in the reverie of how this slaughter had unfolded. For I absolutely relish that they all know me as Jack the Ripper, but here, I am—just Detective Scotts.

Guest Milk

Jessica Gleason

BRIAN TOOK a black Sharpie and labeled the expired carton "Guest Milk." The jug sat curdling in his fridge for months.

Occasionally, he'd break the seal, retching at the sour scent, to toss in rotted carrots or spoiled chunks from forgotten takeout containers. Brian hated waste.

After a night of drunken flirting, Fern accompanied Brian home for anonymous raunchy fornication.

Thirsty post-coitus, she tiptoed to the kitchen. "Guest Milk." *How odd*, she thought, gulping before the rancid taste hit her parched mouth.

Clawing her throat, she gasped, "I should have asked first," before falling down dead, in a pool of bloody vomit.

Never Date Your Ex

Elizabeth Suggs

It was supposed to be a simple emo poetry class, but I'd been tempted and now I've opened a rift in the Shadow Realm. Worst of all—I couldn't stop myself from summoning my ex, Damian. We'd broken up because he was too emotionally unavailable, and he still is. But in that soul-devouring way. He's got that tall, dark, and handsome thing to a T, along with a pair of horns.

I should just close the rift now, but he's looking at me with literally smoldering eyes. He's going to devour me, heart and soul, and I'll let him. Again and again.

defeatism.

Eyes Like Marbles

Kelli Dianne Rule

WE'RE on that golden oak floor, dust-flecked sun streaming through muslin, with so many tumbled candy-colored jewels. Rolling thick, rolling lost—two I'll never forget.

You pluck one eye—your best—and teach me to shoot. A ring scratched in the dust, mibs in a cross—we're playing marbles, knuckled down, aiming to knock them free.

Your eye finds the weakest, those tiny flaws that betray speed.

You, generous, give your other eye to me. Oh, how they roll—seeking, striking—how we gather the mibs and laugh.

You replace your eyes—dimpled, drooping, blood-veined, beaten.

What we give up for youth.

Pool Party

Morgana Price

IT WAITED at the bottom of the pool. The lights created small and flickering reflections in the water across its camouflaged body. It writhed and wriggled in anticipation as the pool finally opened after months of preparation.

After eons of slumber, it awoke unprepared. Humanity took its home, making it flee from its lake. They drained it and built a summer school and camp over it!

How dare they…

Bodies entered the pool. Its tentacles wiggled with glee. Unraveling its massive body, it ascended.

Bursting through the water's surface, it roared an otherworldly rumble. It towered. It grabbed. The water turned red.

Where the Children Wait

K. R. Patterson

EVERYONE KNEW about the abandoned town of children. Why didn't anyone else care? I was sure I'd go in and find corpses instead of children.

I wasn't ready for what I saw. Parts of it looked like a ghost town, but other recent stores were all for children. A candy shop, ice cream, toys. The air smelled of rot mixed with sweets. *Who built these?*

There was no one in sight—dead or alive. Then, footsteps. I turned on the uneven ground and saw a child. A massive snake slithered around his feet.

His smile wasn't natural. "We've been waiting for you."

Best Left Buried

Jordan McClymont

ELSPETH TOOK up necromancy at sixty, and it wasn't until she resurrected her late husband, did she realise the terrible mistake she had made.

"What's for dinner, love?" he'd ask, over and over.

In her nostalgia she'd forgotten just how tiresome relationships can be. Forty years married. You'd think that she'd have had enough. But no, she had to go and bring Big Tam Bills back, just so he could grumble, drink, and moan.

She'll have to take him down memory lane to their favorite cliffs once again, and this time, she won't be making the same mistake of bringing him back.

Ballynahone

Cailín Frankland

YOUR MOTHER TOLD you not to play in the bog. She spoke of its dangers, warned you of the peat mounds giving way, the acid beneath—the bodies long buried but preserved just the same, governed by the undead or the fae or some other ancient spirit. You laughed in her face, called her an old cow, and took off running for the moss—red-cheeked and rain-soaked, reckless as only little boys can be.

You cry for your mother now, clawing at the sky as I pull you under. But it is too late for that, my child. She cannot hear you.

Initial Consequences

Andrew J. Pixton

TIMOTHY CUT a plastic bottle into tiny pieces and threw them into the fast-flowing river.

Cindy said, "Don't, Timmy, that's littering."

"Tell you what, Cindy," he said, carving his initials into a jagged piece. "If someone finds this, they'll know it was me."

He tossed it.

Years later, Timothy sat next to Cindy at their wedding dinner: baked cod from the coast. Cindy choked on the first bite. He performed the Heimlich, but her gagging worsened.

Uncle Jon tried next, and her throat split open. Protruding from her bloody throat was his initialed piece of plastic.

Timothy sobbed. "I'll never litter again."

Broken Promises

H.V. Patterson

BEFORE THEY'D MARRIED, Melanie made George promise he wouldn't look at her on Saturdays from sunrise to sunset. Today was their one-year anniversary, and he'd planned an amazing celebration, but Melanie had still insisted on locking herself in the bathroom!

George decided he wouldn't put up with this secrecy any longer.

He unscrewed the doorknob and opened the bathroom door.

A monster wearing Melanie's face sprawled in the opulent bathtub. George attempted to flee, but agitated tentacles boiled from the water, hauling him into her slimy embrace.

"Why did you have to look?" Melanie sobbed before ripping him into delicious, bite-sized pieces.

Liar, Liar

Natalya Monyok

THEY CALL ME A COMPULSIVE LIAR. I call myself a lover of chaos.

I spend months anonymously messaging Jackson Whittaker. I manipulate him to believe his stepfather, Daniel, is out to kill his precious dog. He thinks the only way to save it is to murder him.

The plan is to meet at Juniper Way, but when I arrive, Jackson isn't there.

Around the corner appears a man dressed in black.

"You thought you could break my family up?"

Daniel pulls out a pistol, aims for my head.

I try to lie my way out, but this time, no one believes me.

26

Snack Time

Brianna Malotke

MYSTERY SURROUNDS the old Victorian manor on Chestnut Lane. The exterior of the run-down painted lady is unimpressive. Your curiosity grows with each step. What lurks behind the doors?

Stories of suspicious disappearances and bodies buried under flowerbeds echo in your mind. You seek the truth. Against all warnings from your parents, with the lightest of touches, you knock.

A little old granny answers. Your fear fades away as she invites you in for snickerdoodles. Her voice is calm, appearance dainty. The deadbolt locks, her wicked grin spreads, revealing rows and rows of monstrous teeth.

The truth is—there are no cookies.

The Fall

Robin Knabel

SHAKING, I close the window. Warm breath condenses into thick mist.

New friends wait below. The ones who dared me to sneak out, to atone for getting them into trouble. My plagiarists.

I'm guilty, too. I left my paper exposed. Inviting them. Brazen.

My parents are awed by my straight-A, curve-smashing prowess.

These rebels won't impress them. Underachievers. Riffraff. "They're bad apples."

But loneliness begets desperation. And poor decisions. I've learned that over many years and many schools.

"Hurry up, bookworm!"

Losing my balance, gravity grasps me.

Lying in the snow, stars fade to black.

Laughter dissipates.

I'm alone again.

Lesson learned.

Lab Rat

AudraKate Gonzalez

SKITTERING FEET ECHOED across the linoleum floor. Frank cowered behind his desk, sweat on his brow. He'd made a huge mistake. *Huge.* The experiment was just supposed to improve the rat's motor functions. Not create a monster. If only he could get to the door, he may be able to make it to safety.

With his escape plan in mind, he darted out from his hiding spot and ran to the door.

His exit was blocked as a giant white figure dropped from the ceiling.

"Leaving so soon?" the lab rat said, white whiskers twitching, and bald tail swishing back and forth.

Rabid

Chris Jorgensen

I SHUT the cabin door as hard as I could, bracing myself against it. The sounds of

growls on the other side meant the beast was still out there. The rustling of cans meant it had

found the trash, looking for food. I locked the door and bolted the small bar, acting

like a great shield against the world.

The heavy creaking on the porch outside made me scurry away to the corner of

the room by the fireplace. The door moaned, bent, and fell to the floor.

Those yellow eyes found me. Strange creatures in the wild are better left alone.

Fishy Homework

Joshua Booker

"FINISH THAT PAPER for more screen time!" Grant's mom shouted from downstairs. Looking around the room for inspiration, Grant's eyes landed on his betta fish, a creamy white male splotched with blue-green.

Write a story where a dumb mom turns into a fish, he typed into ChatBuddy. Out came a tale fifty words short of his assignment, but Grant massaged it to length.

"All done!" he shouted after submitting it on Schoology. No answer. And his phone was still locked.

"Mom! Done!" Motion in the tank caught his eye. Inside was a second betta fish, colored as red as his mother's hair.

Missing Cat

Sara Fitzgerald

DARCY STOOD by the glowing streetlamp and tore the Missing Cat poster off the fraying blue wood.

Mr. Smith ambled out of his home, shaking his cane. "About time you gave up. Your mangy tabby cat always pooped in my yard. I did warn you."

His words cemented the horrible sentiment she'd never see her beloved Harold again. She found the rat poison carelessly thrown in his overflowing trash bin, the same poison she used this morning.

"Good to see you. I baked fresh blueberry muffins." She forced a bright smile. "Want one?"

His mouth watered as his beady eyes bulged. "Yup."

Advantage

Hannah Grace

"You're very mature for eighteen." He pours me another glass of Malbec.

I nod politely, flashing a demure smile.

"Besides, age is just a number and twenty-seven is just a gap. Cheers, darling!" He watches, smirking as I empty my glass.

Brushing my golden hair back he looks dreamily into my eyes "Can I kiss you?"

"Why, of course."

What starts as a passionate kiss grows cold, his face now gaunt and cemented into a silent scream. I drain the bottle next, gazing as he crumbles into rubble. His life force pulses through my veins, putting a pep in my six-hundred-and-eighteen-year-old step.

Trapped

Natalya Monyok

I FLOAT in a barren wasteland of dead stars and broken asteroids.

Darkness swallows me whole.

The escape pod I am trapped in drifts further into uncharted space with each passing day.

I have been stripped of all my achievements and accolades. I am no longer a commanding general leading Earth's army into battle. I am no one. I am nothing.

I have enough food and water to last five years, then my suffering will end. By then, I will surely be insane.

Five years.

I should've died with my men.

I shouldn't have sacrificed them to save myself.

Five more years.

Fastball

Charles Kyd

HE'D ALREADY HIT me on purpose, twice. Fastballs off my helmet. Why? Doesn't matter. You hit a guy in the throat or face with a hundred-mile-an-hour fastball, you might kill him. This time, when he accidentally hung a juicy changeup over the plate, I had all the time I needed to watch it spin, step into it, and—crack.

The thing I remember best is just this red, squishy explosion when it hit his eye. His head really snapped back; he was limp before he even started falling. Of course, I wish he hadn't died—but no, I don't regret that swing.

Circe

Anne Gregg

"*WITCH*" stained my locker in pig's blood.

"Bring him back!" Macy, my school's blonde bombshell, shoved me into my locker.

"What?" I said.

"Don't play dumb you jealous hag. You're the reason Chris is missing."

"Now why would I make your boyfriend disappear?"

"You love him."

I cackled, "I don't."

"You'd be lucky if he looked at you."

"I'd be *lucky*?" I scoffed. "You know what he did!"

"Aww, Ada, why would anyone believe you?"

After school, I wandered through my family's pigsty and poured slop into the bucket. One oinked at me, indignant.

"Cheer up, Chris. Macy will join you soon."

Kafka's Dating Game

Peter L. Harmon

IRVING WASN'T sure what to expect when he signed up for the interspecies dating reality show on the new alien streaming service. He had never done anything like it before, but he had struck out with the earthbound methods. He was looking for love.

But he did actually meet a nice potential mate and they really hit it off, so much so that they spent a wonderful night together.

In the morning, after his stomach began to hurt and saw the movement under his skin, he read up about her planet's mating rituals. That was when the first eggs began to hatch.

The Bookstore Beauty

Robert J. Foster

He walked up to the blonde cashier and winked at her.

"Hey, gorgeous, where are the erotica books?"

"Here."

She mosied behind the Western bookshelf and popped out, wearing a cowgirl hat.

"Howdy, buckaroo!"

Passing the Shakespeare section, she said with an Elizabethan accent, "Nearly there!"

He saw British Literature, looked behind him, saw Western, Comedy ahead.

They approached the comedy aisle, and she transformed into a harlequin. "One section until erotica, goofball!"

Distracted by her bright colors, he missed the next sign. She leapt out of a dark corner and stabbed him.

He bled to death in the Murder Mystery section.

Cactus

Thomas S. Salem

THE KIDNAPPER CORNERED the boy in his dingy apartment. It was just the two of them, and it was well past the boy's bed time.

The boy clutched a green apple and whimpered, "Don't eat my cactus."

"That's an apple, stupid."

"No, it's a cactus——"

The kidnapper snatched the tasty treat from the boy, brought it to his mouth, and chomped into it. Saliva oozed from his lips, but he only panicked when he tasted blood.

So much blood.

The kidnapper yanked the apple free. He could see razor blades embedded in it.

"I told you not to eat my cactus!"

Failure to Comply

Cailín Frankland

"THIS IS FOR YOUR OWN GOOD," they say as they strip us bare, scrub our skin raw. "You are sick, compromised—we cannot trust you with your clothes, your dirt, your freedom. We will take care of you. Stop resisting."

There are new words for everything here: our cages are bedrooms, our handcuffs bracelets. They are not drugging us, strapping us to cold steel tables, and pulling out our teeth —they are stabilizing, de-escalating, practicing harm reduction.

They think they have subdued us, declawed our spirits with our bodies. But they forget—the mad are many, and we do not go gently.

Perfect Friend, Designed

Steve Capone, Jr.

WHEN THE MAN who looks like me, talks like me, and resembles me in all his physical features steps into the light, I look him over. He's been gone all day.

Blood dribbles from his fingertips and splashes on the floor at his feet.

I am struck dumb.

"We get to do what we want," he says, in my voice.

I must make a sound because he explains. "Always a perfect alibi. You are doing what you wish, and I am doing what I wish."

I find my voice. "But I made you to be like me."

"I am. In every way."

Disappearance

Ethan Stewart

KATIE WALKED into the bookstore with her head down, ignoring playful nudges from her sister, Anna. It was hard to share her warm demeanor. Everyone was leaving, and no one saw it.

"Katie?"

Katie looked up, her chest tightening. "Please, no," she said, tears running down her cheeks, "Not you too!" Anna looked down at her fading body, then made eye contact. They embraced as she disappeared, and passersby continued on their business, without a single glance her way. *Gone. All gone.* Her best friend, her boyfriend, and now even her sister. All her friends had vanished, and no one could see.

The Good Employee

Jenny Castro

Marketing Director Ms. Taylor summoned Mandy, the marketing intern, to her office: "Darling, I need your eyes." *She needs help on another presentation?* Mandy sighed and walked to the oversized and overly white office.

The day had dragged on, filled with demanding deadlines and frustratingly complex data, leaving her vision blurred. When the work was finally complete, Ms. Taylor moved away from the computer screen, her face softening with satisfaction. The work was done, and Mandy sat staring into the darkness. Her blue eyes, now shining from the boss's sockets, had not only done the job but also looked great on her.

Judgement Night

Jordan McClymont

WRAPPED IN FORBIDDEN SORCERY, Inquisitor Rake cuts through a thick forest. After tonight, they won't be laughing behind her back in court.

Deeper in—disturbed by power—the Dead rise from their graves.

Fresh blood. Rake's hunt draws to a close. *So soon?* Rake grins, then leaps.

She has them. They cower before a woman malformed by magic. Rake forges a sickle to slice them like the weeds—

"No!"

The Dead swarm her like wolves. Her magic—sweet like the sun. This was supposed to be her moment. The night she proved them all wrong.

When she arrives in Hell, they're laughing.

Toots the Clown

Jessica Gleason

ELENA'S SKIN TORE, her knees scraping the gritty playground pavement. She stood, brushing pebbles from her wounds, while blood streamed down her shins and stained her new white socks.

Eyes wide, she looked up at the clown statue, confused by her stumble. Eyeing it suspiciously, and remembering how she'd defaced it back in grade school, she shuddered. The mascot's perma-smile always unnerved her, but the playground was the quickest path home.

She kicked the clown in anger, waking Toots, and stuck her tongue out before hobbling home.

Elena's pulse quickened when she heard the distinct shuffle of comically large shoes behind her.

Your Antagonist

Jonathan Reddoch

I'M THE ANTAGONIST. I slay queens. I rip what you sow.

Fueled with grimm sorrow, driven by cruel backstory, I stalk your dreams at dusk and haunt your steps at dawn.

You're the protagonist. You pray while I prey. You freak and flee and fight.

In stories old, the protagonist is forever victorious against the vile villain.

But this isn't a fantasy story. Nor a fairytale. Not a romance, comedy, or adventure.

Sass and sin! It's the night's tale.

I put the *agony* in the protagonist. Only bloody gore awaits our tormented hero.

It's a ghost story. And you're the ghost.

Cozy and Quiet

Elizabeth Suggs

MAYA LOWERED HER PHONE. The description called the hostel "cozy and quiet." It was quiet with it being far off the grid, but cozy? *As if.* The place looked like it had been condemned more than a year ago.

She was just about to leave a scathing review when Derek, a blond almost too pale dreamboat approached her. He'd been here for a while, but he was waiting to be invited inside. Seeing as it was late and there wasn't another hostel for miles, a night alone with him didn't seem so bad. Especially when he smiled.

So, she invited him inside.

Ghost House

Paul Lonardo

THE SOUL of a rich man's wife haunts the house where she died. The anguished man attempts to allay her suffering by expanding the home, adding a thousand rooms filled with spirits of the dead so she would not be lonely.

He spent his fortune creating a mansion. Upon his death, his grieved spirit was condemned to the same humble abode. However, because of the number of rooms and the endless maze of corridors, his spirit is unable to find his beloved wife. The man's plaintive cries of loneliness can be heard as he wanders through the enormous house looking for her.

Fine Print

Jo Birdwell

Robert chased fame and fortune his whole life, yearning for popularity, no matter how he got it: get rich quick schemes, leaning on friends' successes, stepping on anyone in his way, social media influencing. All to no avail. He just wanted to be known.

Desperate, he stood at the crossroads, reciting his invocation. Ol' Scratch appeared, contract in hand. Robert signed, eager to receive the renown he desired.

As he laid down the pen, a fiery pit opened beneath him.

In Hell, all eyes were finally on him. His suffering would be legendary.

Robert was never one to read the fine print.

Bad Tipper

Ace Mack

ANDY SCANNED for seats at the stage. The bartender held up two fingers, turning his hand back and forth. Andy nodded. A pair of shots and lunch plates arrived, followed by two exotic dancers.

Seafood pasta dripped out of his mouth onto a stack of Benjamins. Chomping his last shrimp, Andy tossed bills at one dancer, then turned to leave. The other protested, "Ya can't just tip her. Ya owe mi!"

"That was garbage."

"To soot duppy! To soot!"

"Keep your island curse, whore." Reaching down, his pocket was burning him. Instead of keys or cash, he found just flakes of ash.

Angel on the Outward Side

Keyra K. Allred

"Trick or treat!"

Brandon hated Halloween. He hated the stupid decorations and waiting for obnoxious little kids to clomp up the stairs, shouting at him for free treats. Here was another one. A waifish blonde girl, swathed in rainbow tulle and haphazard fairy wings. Her angelic smile infuriated him.

"I choose *trick*," he snapped. *Might be worth a laugh.*

Cocking her head to the side, wide smile baring pointed teeth. She nodded.

"Creepy kid," Brandon said, leaning away. His final words before the despised orange and black decorations turned toward him as one, leaped as one, and swallowed him down as one.

The Fantasy Book of Evil

Devin Guignard

LITTLE SOFIA CAMPBELL despised loud noises—especially when they interrupted her reading. Her father somehow always knew she was reading when he ran the clanging laundry, the grinding dishwasher, and worst, the roaring vacuum cleaner. She hated its sound, wishing anything to stop the shrieking clatter.

That morning, she was reading a fantasy book called *Necronomicon for Kids*.

A passage materialized, instructing to clear her mind and recite *Oajah-zhrah-j'ai-frokv-bwioh'k-l'gehb*, and the first thing she wished would occur.

It was only fantasy!

For her father turned on the vacuum cleaner, and she recited...

She never saw the vacuum cleaner again.

Or her father.

Frog

Mae Thorn

CALVIN PUSHED the scalpel down into the frog's dead flesh. He shifted as rotten liquid squirted towards him.

"Next time, Calvin, don't be late. Don't make excuses about the life of frogs," said his teacher, Miss Albright.

Calvin peeled the flesh away from the sternum. A little frog hand twitched, and he cried out.

"What is it this time?"

"It moved!"

"Nonsense," Miss Albright said. "It can't move."

The frog's glazed eyes became wide and black. And was it smiling? Can frogs smile?

"What…?"

The creature's open torso grew to a void of darkness. Calvin and Miss Albright knew nothing but oblivion.

Fly Swatter

Makayla Nielson

A FLY BUZZED near Watson's ear. He swatted it, making contact. It landed on its back and spun helplessly in a circle on the ground.

"Disgusting." Watson mocked.

Henderson, *that big-headed, pompous, goody-two-shoes,* scooped up the bug. "Your wing is bent." He flicked his wrist, muttering a Mending Spell. "There you go, little fella."

The creature pulsed and glowed red, expanding in size.

Watson grimaced. It wasn't a mending spell. It was a bolstering spell.

The insect cocked its head, and its compound eyes locked on Watson. The cow-sized fly swatted Watson, plastering him to the ground.

The fly seemed to smile.

It's Just Your Voice

Selene Ibarra Rubio

Niquel never liked her daughter, Kira's, constant rambling. She would have given anything to stop the nonsense about the garden rocks and bright insects. When Niquel came across a scientific trial that limited a person's speech, allowing them to speak only five thousand words every day, she immediately accepted.

Niquel relished the quiet. The implantation that latched Kira's mangled jaw shut with teeth-breaking force, was worth it, she thought. Until one dark night: Kira, with a needle and thread, crawled into her mother's room while she slept. If she could speak five thousand words daily forever, then Niquel wouldn't speak at all.

Alien Artifact

K. R. Patterson

As the dean lay chained on a cold metal table with a snaking probe up his ass, he cursed Professor Sanchez. They'd planned to fire him for telling the students he could identify an artifact's origin by touch alone. He'd even said the latest one wasn't from Earth. The dean had thought Sanchez was crazy, but he wasn't laughing now.

To discredit him, he'd joined a dig. When Sanchez asked, "Wanna touch it?" the dean had smirked and pressed his palm to the artifact's surface.

It pulsed.

Now, underground, Sanchez turned. "You should've listened," he said, as the probe began to hum.

Homestead Horror

Jayne Ann Osborne

SARAH SURVEYED HER NEW SURROUNDINGS. She loved it already—the smell of animals, the sound of honeybees, the warm sunshine.

She had always dreamed of homesteading. When fate finally came to call, it was even better than she'd imagined, but she just needed to lose the voices and rhythmic beeping in her head. She couldn't quite make sense of either and didn't care to.

"You coming?" Grandpa called.

"Where to?"

"Out to pasture," he replied.

As she followed, the scene faded into one long, final beep. One last whisper.

"Pull the plug."

The sound of her weeping family faded into the background.

Practice Makes Perfect

P.S. Tom

PROFESSOR HUNTS STEPS OUT of his classroom, takes a breath of crisp autumn air, and begins to walk through the woods. After a few minutes, he hears branches snapping behind him. He quickens his pace to a jog. A loud crack and thud force him to the ground. Standing over him is a wolflike creature. It leans in, jaws open.

"Wait!" shouts Hunts.

The creature freezes.

"I could smell you from the moment I left my office, and you've been clumsy this whole time. You've not been practicing your hunting basics!" Hunts shouts while furiously shaking his finger.

"Let's do it again!"

Casper Bridge

J.B. Corso

A SULFUR-LADEN RIFT out of Hell opens up, spreading its ominous presence through a rural wooded area. Its gashed form pushes through a chasm under the Casper Bridge.

The bloodied deaths of thirteen joggers and a patrolling county deputy stain the road's bookends. A trembling detective quits after returning from the overpass.

One humid afternoon, Thomas's morbid curiosity was piqued. The young public works employee hobbles home with quivering fingers and a blood-splattered face. His wife becomes frantic, begging him for an answer. She caresses his hand.

Thomas' blank eyes stare through her. "Their claws are opening the rift further every minute."

Bet

Jacek Wilkos

MARTIN MADE a bet with his friends he could spend the entire night at the abandoned St. Dymphna Psychiatric Hospital. Neither stories of hauntings nor "danger of collapse" signs deterred him. He had a reputation to live up to.

Standing before once-white, massive wooden doors, he felt his buddies' eyes on him, but he didn't turn around. He went in.

His friends returned just before dawn. They went inside to find Martin. They feared the worst—finding him possessed, catatonic, or ritually murdered.

The reality turned out to be prosaic.

They found him under a pile of concrete debris from collapsed stairs.

The Blood Moon

Paul Lonardo

I SAW my new neighbor lying out on her deck at 3 a.m. She was wearing a red bikini, her pale skin shimmering under the light of the Hunter's Moon.

I had been dying to meet her since she moved in. I went over to say hello. She asked me to put lotion on her back.

Now I lay next to her, unable to move. She pressed the skin near the holes in my neck, dabbing the blood that leaked out onto the tips of her fingers and applied it to her body. It soaked into her flesh, giving her eternal life.

An Ending for Agnes

Robert J. Foster

AGNES ENTERED the only vehicle in the hospital parking garage.

A gun jabbed her side. Greg shouted, "Turn left!"

She obeyed, driving toward a vacant lot.

"Pull over!"

She stopped, facing a brick wall.

Agnes grinned. She looked into the man's furious eyes and pressed her foot to the accelerator.

"Stop the car, bitch!" Greg shoved the gun harder into her side and gritted his teeth.

Agnes said, "The doctor told me today—I'm terminal." She pushed the pedal down—harder. "If my time's up, then I'm bringing you with me, *bitch*."

Greg's eyes widened.

He hadn't known he was terminal too.

Fortune

M. L. Smythe

Jared couldn't believe his luck.

Normally, finding a corpse on the way to work would be an omen, but Jared found something that he knew would change his life forever.

A winning lottery ticket. Ten million dollars.

Was it wrong for him to take it? Maybe. He had done his due diligence: called the police, waited for them to arrive before leaving the body. He considered this his payment. After all, the corpse wouldn't need the money.

Out of his periphery, came a deep, black shadow which spread until it encompassed his entire vision. He couldn't breathe.

He couldn't believe his luck.

Biscuit Revenge

Corinne Pollard

Dwight drizzled crumbs into a trap. The rodent would pay for devouring his favorite biscuits.

His wife protested, but he paid no attention.

One night his phone beeped, claiming the trap had captured something. He scrambled to the kitchen in his pajamas, but the trap was empty. He gritted his teeth as squeaks mocked him.

Dwight grabbed a mop and scanned the tiled floor, unable to return to bed until he'd squished it.

"Die! Die! Die!"

From their cozy bedroom, his wife heard him. She smiled, sighing before helping herself to a biscuit—*his* biscuits—while unaware of the added tasteless poison.

One Last House

Elizabeth Rayne

THROUGH THE HOLLOW eyes of his ghoul mask, Caleb glimpsed a light in the window of the supposedly haunted Ashworth house and a large bowl of cellophane-wrapped caramels waiting on the porch.

He grabbed a handful, stuffing them into his pillowcase. He lingered behind his older sister to sneak one into his mouth. The candy, though sweet, had a strange, metallic aftertaste. Feeling dizzy, he stumbled over a rock in the yard.

On his knees, he saw the rock was actually an old gravestone. "Here lies Jessamine Ashworth, born 1868, died 1879," it read, "The only thing she ever wanted was friends."

An Awkward Encounter

Keyra K. Allred

MULBERRY DREADLOCKS FLOAT wildly among the steaming foam, intrigued amber eyes glowing. Silver flashes just beneath the water's surface. She winks and I'm hers. Lips curving in a smile, bright against her rich, brown skin, and I wonder if I have something on my face. Sinuously gliding, she's crossing the open space between us. Long, slim fingers slide up my arm, leaving promise in their frozen wake. So close. So utterly close. Her frigid breath grazes my neck. Grimacing around razor-sharp teeth, she bites down, allowing my blood to swirl madly.

Consciousness fading, one thought remains: *Why did I join this gym?*

Impressive Credentials

Gregory Meece

ATTRACTED BY INTREPID INNOVATIONS' high salaries, Bill realized his bland resume would never land him a position with the company boasting, "We're the apex in scientific discovery."

I'll just embellish a bit, he thought, and began inventing experiences meant to impress: geological drilling beneath the polar ice caps, gator dodging while studying the Everglades mangroves, and tracking aggressive wildebeests in their Tanzanian habitat.

Pretty "intrepid" stuff!

Impressed with his thrilling background, the search committee agreed Bill was the right man for the job—one Bill regretted as soon as the test rocket launched him outside a world he would never see again.

Helping Hand

Peter L. Harmon

In the big city, out on the street, Cynthia needed help. Her books were way too heavy to carry alone. She asked a passing man for a hand, but he just pointed to his phone.

Cynthia would have rewarded his kindness, she had that power, but instead, she shook her head and muttered.

The man woke up in the middle of the night and he wasn't feeling so grand. His feet were hands, his hands were hands, each finger was a hand. Hands grew out of his neck and covered his mouth and ears.

Now, he finally had a hand to spare.

Shipping Error

Alex Child

RILEY'S CRATE unexpectedly opened in the cargo plane. He slammed it shut, but the burly forklift driver already saw him.

"This is the only way I'll afford Cancun!" Riley hissed.

The driver said nothing.

The plane ascended, Riley's carton wedged tight among the others. Upon landing, he watched a forklift pick up his box, move him onto a truck, and unload him in a warehouse.

"You disrespect the shipping industry, you pay the price," a voice growled.

Riley glanced through the peephole and saw the same forklift driver. He pleaded as his box was surrounded by crates, sealing his fate in darkness.

Library Etiquette

Gregory Meece

"Please don't bend the book's cover—you'll crack its spine," said Miss Julien.

Forty years behind the circulation desk, Hoover High's wizened librarian safeguarded her precious books.

Toby callously twisted the cover until loosened pages fluttered onto Miss Julien's feet. "Nobody reads these things anymore," he said, tossing the book like trash.

Summoning unexpected strength, Miss Julien drove her weight into the towering bookshelf. Toby cowered as a stack of encyclopedias crashed upon him. She called emergency services.

The paramedic carefully supported Toby's neck. "No limb movement."

"I always tell the boys not to climb on the stacks," said the concerned librarian.

Sundown Town

Russell Evans

"You shoulda known better than to get caught in a sundown town!" the sheriff yelled at the shadow racing through the trees, gun drawn.

It was 1970, but damn if he'd let tradition die on his watch. The flashlight caught the dark figure splashing to the other side of the creek. He thought, *good, no witnesses to a good ole fashioned lynching.*

Suddenly, they were gone. I took a step forward, but stumbled and fell hard, my foot trapped by a root.

Footsteps approached… lumbering… staggering… inhuman strangled moans. Dark eyeless corpses grasped me. I screamed as the flashlight dimmed like sundown.

Noodlemas Eve

Jessica Gleason

"Marco, you aren't observing Holiday this year?"

"No, I'm tired of being ignored. I've never felt the blessing of his noodly appendages."

Sven considered his friend, looking him up and down, "Hmmm… you are much too tall, but we don't question the Flying Spaghetti Monster. Not even Steve himself knows what quob may do if you forsake them."

"Are you listening to yourself? Stupid quob is fictional!"

"You shouldn't say that." Sven shied away from his wayward friend in horror as marinara streamed in from the windows. Sven was blessed to witness a miracle as Marco boiled and drowned, a tomato-flavored death.

The Deal in the Dark

Addison Hope

A SQUELCH RIPS from the man's neck when I tear the knife from his throat. I drop his limp body to the forest floor, exhausted. Covered in blood, I gaze up at the stars in the midnight sky.

"It's done," I say, waiting.

I hear rustling from behind me and turn around. There it stands, nearly seven feet tall, stick-thin, its antlers towering like trees. It stares, then walks past me, picks up the carcass, and devours it. It truly is disgusting to watch.

As the creature rips yet another tendon from the carcass, I sigh. *What did I sign up for?*

My Pleasure

Jonathan Redddoch

"YOUR DRINK, SIR," the Chick Fill-Up worker said, smiling broadly. His nametag read *Tanner*.

"Uhhh, thanks," the teen snickered.

"My pleasure."

"Your *pleasure*?" he cringed.

"Will there be anything else, sir?"

The teen pushed his drink off the table, splattering its icy contents across the linoleum. "You can pleasure yourself by getting me another pop."

Tanner returned with a fresh soda and even wider grin.

"Thanks."

"My *pleassssure*."

Later, the teen woke up strapped to a chair, every orifice slowly draining blood.

He saw Tanner's crooked smile, his outfit stained a darker shade of red.

"What's happening?" the teen muttered.

"My pleasure."

Lucy

F. Malanoche

JOHNATHAN SPENT every night for the last month in the library where he could have a clear view of the front desk, looking at the only thing he wanted to checkout: the librarian whose vibrant red hair obscured her face. Still, her milky white legs stirred something in him. Her hair bounced as if she were always moving through water.

Realizing the library would close soon, he walked up to her, prepared to ask her out. She looked at him, curved her crimson lips upward, and bared her fangs. It would be a dinner date, and he would be the main course.

Invitation to the Void

Robert J. Foster

THE VOID SWIRLED on the lab floor.

"I'm not going," said Wilhelm.

"You must," said Einar.

"Anything could be in there," said Wilhelm.

"That's why you need to go in. Find out what 'anything' is," said Einar.

Wilhelm stepped forward, shook, and dropped into the void.

Colors swallowed him, spun him, and fogged his mind. It felt alive and insatiably greedy.

"Let me out!" Wilhelm screamed.

"Impossible," whispered the void inside his mind. "But you may invite another."

"Everything okay in there?" shouted Einar.

Wilhelm stared at the swirling colors around him, his eternal trap, and said, "Yes. It's wonderful. Join me."

Not His Reflection

Elizabeth Suggs

I SIGNED up for Mr. Gregor's chemistry lab because Matt, the hot and broody TA, kept looking at me. Classic goth—long dark hair, always in black. But it wasn't him I watched the first day. It was his reflection. It stared, even when he didn't.

I thought I was losing it until I saw his reflection in my bedroom mirror that night.

I reached for it.

It touched back.

No—it pulled me through.

Now I'm trapped in a realm of endless darkness and silence.

Matt's reflection still holds me. Still watches.

He wanted me here.

If only I could scream.

The Life of Thomas McGuire

M. L. Smythe

Tom knew he must be losing his mind.

He had received the manuscript in his email: *The Life of Thomas McGuire*. It was a common enough name, a coincidence.

When he started reading, however, he grew angry: his entire life written in the document in front of him. Every moment. How?

He was sick as he read about the exact moment that he was in right now: at his desk, reading this exact manuscript.

He agonized over whether to continue reading. Would there be anything else?

He read about his future; next week, then next month; then nothing. Why was there nothing?

Provoked

Makayla Nielson

THE WHISPERING of shifting sand echoed through the otherwise empty room, emanating from a cloth-covered box.

Watson creeped over and ripped away the cloth, startling the sinuous snake within. The scaly creature lunged at the glass, its fangs knocking against the cage with a grotesque crack.

He shuddered, *slimy good for nothin'*...

He banged the glass and the snake shrunk away.

"What're you gonna do about it?" Watson sneered.

The snake coiled and sprung, breaking free of the tank. Its fangs sunk into Watson's bicep.

His vision blurred, and he dropped to the ground.

Henderson stood above him. "You found my pet!"

A Grave of My Own

Madison Parker

"Just one more. One more, Fossor," I swore to myself.

In the cover of night, I dragged my shovel up the hill where I had spotted a freshly dug grave.

Times had been hard, and I needed to put food on the table. It's not like they needed their trinkets anymore.

Quickly and quietly I dug, until I hit the wooden box.

Prying the lid open, I paused to notice the lack of smell.

The casket was empty! Confused, I lit my lantern and held it up to the slab of stone to see who it was meant for.

"Fossor Edward Moros."

Cracking Nuts

Corinne Pollard

"You couldn't keep it in your pants."

She stood beside the bed, leaning over her husband, while holding a wooden figurine. The wood-carved soldier was a drummer from her precious collection with golden trimmed uniform, boots, and hat. She stroked its furry beard as it glared with a lipless grin.

"I gave you a second chance, and this is how you repay me?! At Christmas!"

With a clunk, the soldier's mouth fell open, but instead of teeth, spikes glistened. She'd modified it.

Her husband struggled against his restraints, whimpering behind the duct tape.

"Let's see if *your* nuts crack."

The nutcracker descended.

Reaper

Natalya Monyok

In the graveyard, Maya sobbed tears of blood. Claire screamed and rushed to her sister, but Maya shoved her away.

"Don't come near."

Claire watched in horror as Maya's veins turned black, protruding against porcelain skin. "What's happening to you?"

Maya raised her gaze to the heavens. "God is here."

"Please, I don't understand, just let me go get mom."

At the mention of their mother, Maya snapped back to Claire. "Mom was the one who killed me, ignorant child."

She stalked past her to the graveyard's entrance, her sights set on the town.

"But it is Vengeance who has awakened me."

Fender Bender

Joshua Booker

BUT DID YOU DIE? reads the bumper sticker on a beat-up Chevrolet Malibu up ahead. It was a sentiment very familiar to Oscar, who always downplayed his kids' worries. When they would come to him with problems, he would say they were overreacting. "Wait until you have to pay rent," was a household adage.

A text message pops up on his phone from his daughter:
Omg dad this project is killing me
Calm dow–he types before colliding with the Malibu. He flew through the windshield and crashed to the pavement, staring straight into the bumper sticker, paralyzed from the neck down.

Office Love

Jenny Castro

JESSICA SAT beside the most handsome man at the office, his blue eyes a constant distraction. She felt a thrill every time they worked together, the energy of their conversations electrifying.

In a moment of unbridled passion, she confessed her love, choosing to accept an affair even though he was already married.

To her surprise, he answered, "An affair? I want to marry you!" Overjoyed, that he loved her too. She acted impulsively.

Later, alone under the harsh office lights, she felt a sharp pain. A gaping hole in her chest. She had offered her heart, and he had taken it gladly.

Past the Cemetery

Debra Birdwell Winkler

Two girls hesitated at the corner of the cemetery fence.

I greeted them, "Good evening."

"Hello," squeaked the first girl. "Would you walk us past the graveyard?"

"Of course," I replied. "It's a bit spooky at dusk."

"Yeah," they echoed.

I smiled.

"Thank you," the first girl said.

"Are you new to the area?" I asked.

The second one responded. "We've just started university here and live in the dorms."

At the gate, the first girl inquired, "Where do you live?"

I nodded. "Over there two rows down, third tombstone on the right."

I have never seen two people skedaddle so fast.

Clear-Cut

Alex Child

DR. DUBEC WAS FASCINATED by the art of self-surgery, chaining his subjects until they agreed to perform. His newest subject, Rory, was directed to make a daily incision, and only after becoming completely covered in scars, would he be free. Today's cut was the last. Rory glide the blade delicately down his eyelid, savoring the moment as instructed by Dubec.

Vacant eyes glared back before Dr. Dubec barked, "Cut your eyes too. Cut them now." Rory grimaced as he pierced his right cornea. Tears blurred his fading vision as crimson streaks trailed over countless scars.

He never should have trusted Dr. Dubec.

Until Death Do We Part

Sara Fitzgerald

MICHAEL HAULED his luxury luggage up the ornate spiral staircase. The mansion was cold and eerie. It was just after midnight. Not a soul in sight.

"You're such a psycho," his friend said, laughing. "I still can't believe you poisoned your bride, stole her inheritance, and actually went on the honeymoon."

Michael chuckled. "I did the old hag a favor, putting her out of her misery. She was such a homely thing. Better go."

He strode into the master bedroom, where the stench assaulted his senses, a cold hand gripped him, dragging him.

"Until death do we part," his bride's corpse whispered.

Smart Home for Stupid Humans

Michaela Rae

DUSTIN TORE open the packaging of MiMi2. It was sleek and more intuitive than MiMi1, which he immediately tossed in the SmartBin.

He set up MiMi2 to manage all the other smart devices, including his security system.

The home was a bastion of productivity until one evening. Dustin commanded, "MiMi2, dispose of the trash."

The command reverberated throughout the house as each device turned on, "Initiating directive, disposing of the trash."

A muffled voice echoed from the SmartBin, unprovoked but chillingly clear. MiMi1 said, "Dispose of the humanoid trash."

All devices in the house repeated in chorus, "Confirmed, disposing of humanoid trash."

I Would Do Anything for
Love, But...

F. Malanoche

BERENICE RECLINED until she comfortably stared into the soft
eyes of Nicolas. He swept his bangs over his ear. The dental
light shone behind his manly silhouette. Her knees drew in
tight against the tingling in her lower half.

Berenice had been sweet on Nicolas since they first met
in sixth grade. He was beautiful but dumb. She helped him
when he had trouble with any class. The more he needed
her, the more she was around.

Now she found herself as his patient at dental school.
His drill inched toward her. This too would be a lesson only
she would learn.

Academic Integrity

Thomas S. Salem

Nursing student Kimberly Root sat in the dean's office, sipping her lemon water.

Dean Hampton smiled. "Congratulations, you passed the final with a 92."

Kimberly sighed. She had gotten away with it.

"However, the test wasn't designed to be passed. It was created to find cheaters."

She spit out the water.

He placed his hand on her shoulder. "The University prides itself on academic integrity, Miss Root. Please, keep drinking. It's a little something to slow your heart rate just enough so you lose consciousness. You may or may not feel the medical students using you for their surgical final this afternoon."

It Means Nothing

Anne Gregg

I GAVE the void my dog, and it was happy. My wife did not believe Biscuit ran away, but she had no proof. She said she went into my "awful" lab to look for her but found nothing. The void asked for her when she visited, so I pushed her in and wept. Then my daughter snuck into the lab as I was working, and she had to go too. I hugged her goodbye. She kicked and screamed. But the void needed her, and the void is more important than any mortal.

Finally, I gave the void myself, and it rejected me.

Cruelty-Free

Jo Birdwell

CRUELTY-FREE. That's how Stephen marketed his skincare products to the women. His lab rats disagreed. Imprisoned in a makeshift lab, in the basement of his home, in tiny cages, they were covered in bald patches, rashes, and bloody lesions. They were shown no kindness.

Stephen had a new formula to try. Before heading to bed, he injected each of them with his new serum, anxious to see the morning outcome.

Overnight, the rats doubled in size and strength, tenaciously tearing through their wire cages. What was left of Stephen was found the following afternoon: a bed full of blood, bones, and innards.

Devil's Dream

Amber Buckley

THE INSOMNIA NEVER STOPPED. It clung to Alex's body and mind, heavy as wet cloth. His eyes glazed over in the blue glow of the television.

A monotonous religious "documentary" played—God, Jesus, Eve, all the familiar figures. Then the Devil appeared, raging at God before turning to face Alex through the screen.

"I'll let you rest when you kill them all."

The Devil's eyes locked on his. "Alex," he said, "finish what I called you to do. I'm always here. Reminding you."

That was the truth of Alex's insomnia:

Some voices don't want to be silenced.

They want to be obeyed.

Tall Tale

Kelli Dianne Rule

CHUPACABRA. Swamp ape. Bigfoot. I tell them I've seen them all. They laugh. Jokes on them, my stories earn free drinks. I can sure spin a yarn.

What they don't know is, I caught one. Beats me what it is. It's hairy. Small as a child, grunts like a hog. It isn't distressed, just looks at me. It creeps me out, so I cover its cage with a blanket. Hasn't begged for food, so I don't offer. Gotta eat something. Waiting it out.

They found my body shishkebabed on a saw palmetto blade. Fucker didn't even shroud me. Still. Who's laughing now?

Mike Will Have Questions

J.B. Corso

My baby burped her first flame during breakfast. A brief flash over my second cup of coffee. Little Jacqueline and I stare at each other with surprise. She smiles. The brief odor of her sulfur breath lingers between us. A moment of undeniable truth set to scorch my marriage. *How will I explain this to Mike?*

Another flame burp. Mike will have questions. Assumptions. Accusations. My lies about refusing the fire demon's advances will come to an end today.

His footsteps echo through the hallway around an extended yawn. I rub my swollen belly. Mike's weekend will begin with two uncomfortable confessions.

My Family Legacy

Debra Birdwell Winkler

A THUNDERSTORM RAGES as I pull under the portico of my family's ancestral home. One candle lights the front hall, casting eerie shadows.

Momma looks old and tired as she approaches. "It's time, my love."

"But…"

She places her ornate turquoise necklace, no longer bright, around my neck.

"You knew you couldn't escape, dearest. This is your legacy," Momma whispers, fading into the shadows.

I know what to do. I touch the stone and it sparkles.

Immediately, the house lights up. Sunshine shimmers on the marble floor. My ancestors hover around.

Now, I'm responsible for my family, and I can never leave!

Omega Beta Monster

AudraKate Gonzalez

ALL I HAVE to do is kiss Grody Gertrude and I'm instantly a member of Alpha Lambda Kappa. It should be easy, but I can see the plaque on her teeth from across the candlelit dinner I prepared.

"You look beautiful tonight." A lie. She smells like she fell in a lake.

Gertrude smiles, and I almost cringe. Better get this over with. I lean closer, eyes closed and lips puckered.

"You picked the wrong girl to trick," Gertrude hisses. Her tongue stretches out of her mouth, wrapping around my neck, as she pulls me into the dark tunnel of her mouth.

Fingers

Jacek Wilkos

PLAYING ON THE LAWN, little Timmy noticed something slithering out of the sewer grate like an earthworm.

He approached it. It was a finger. A very long finger with a smiley painted on its tip. It was so long that its base disappeared in the darkness of the sewer grate. The finger turned left and right, faced Timmy, and bowed. This amused the boy. Another "smiling" finger emerged from the grate next to the first one, swinging side to side.

Timmy was so fascinated, he didn't notice the sewer manhole behind his back slowly moving and a slender, taloned hand crawling out.

Returned to Me

Jonathan Reddoch

THERE SHE WAS on the sandy shore, in her golden bikini. My long-lost everything, only she was wholly without whit of warmth.

She had been a ten. Now… a negative two might be overly generous.

She washed ashore, bloated, festering, infested with hungry crabs.

Her lidless eyes stared at me, judging me for letting her drown.

I could have saved her, but I was too drunk, my back was turned, and then she was gone, stolen by swollen waves.

But my faithless prayers had been answered!

The angry sea mercilessly returned my tempest-tossed love.

We embraced, reunited, never to be separate again.

Late-Night Forensics Lab

Elizabeth Suggs

I SIGNED up for *Late-Night Forensics* to boost my resume. The class runs late in the "haunted" lab, so few students dare enroll. I don't believe the ghost stories, even when I hear eerie laughter down the dark halls. Ryan, the charming night custodian, insists it's nonsense.

He invites me to meet him late—when it's just us tangled in shadows.

When my professor catches me alone in the closet, Ryan's nowhere to be seen. It's just me. Naked. Cold.

Turns out the university hasn't had a late-night custodian since the last one died twenty-three years earlier cleaning a toxic lab experiment.

Generative Assignation

Steve Capone Jr.

THE ASSIGNMENT: "What will the future hold vis-a-vis the app economy?"

Thirty minutes to a midnight deadline, energy depleted from ADHD web searches run amok—Colin's situation was dire. EssayGen4.0 skulked in a separate tab like a vampire bat awaiting prey in his closet, but he'd wanted to do the work himself.

11:50.

Who am I kidding?

The impossibility of the task overcame his scruples. Maybe just a hint. Colin toggled tabs and typed: "What does the future hold?"

The response slithered, false hesitation. "5:00 a.m. MST."

No shit, Sherlock.

Without additional prompting, a second line followed the first: "Time of death."

Just Like Your Mother

Ashley Huyge

"You're just like your mother," he muttered, more to himself than to me.

I'd asked him repeatedly—he'd say *nagged* him—to pick his socks up off the floor.

He never knew my mother, but he knew what most girls fear. What if we adopt our mothers' picky little quirks?

He didn't know my mother. He didn't know her strange habits. How she'd invite repairmen into the basement. The way she'd cleave the meat from their bones. How carefully she'd dispose of their vans. I admired her. She was brave.

Sometimes I wish I was more like her. That would teach him.

In the Pursuit of Beauty

Natalya Monyok

EM SCRUBBED at her face in the shower. Flakes of skin swirled down the drain. Her face was on fire, so she thought the cold water would help, but it only made it worse.

She wrapped a towel around her chest and went to the vanity. She wiped the condensation off the mirror.

When she saw herself, she unleashed a blood-curdling shriek.

Half her face was missing. The skin was completely gone, revealing the raw dermis layer beneath.

All Em wanted was to be pretty like the other girls

She never should have let that man sell her a black-market skincare acid.

Author Bios

Elizabeth Suggs

Elizabeth Suggs is the co-owner of indie publisher Collective Tales Publishing, founder of Editing Mee, and President of the Horror Writers Association's Utah Chapter. She is the author of multiple award-winning stories, including "Into the Dark" (from the *Collective Darkness* anthology), which became an Amazon bestseller, and "Technicolor Tears," which earned second place in the Quills Short Story Contest. Elizabeth is also a book reviewer (EditingMee.com), a popular bookstagrammer, and a cosplayer (@ElizabethSuggsAuthor). When not immersed in books, she's practicing yoga or traveling the world.

Jonathan Reddoch

Jonathan Reddoch is the co-owner of Collective Tales Publishing and a prolific writer, editor, and publisher. He specializes in sci-fi, fantasy, romance, and especially horror. While well-known for his flash fiction, he also writes poetry and short stories. He's been working on his epic sci-fi novel for over a decade—and hopes to finish it in this lifetime. Originally from Southern California, he now resides in Salt

Lake City. His work appears in *Deluxe Darkness*, *Darkness 101: Lessons Were Learned*, and *This Isn't the Place*. Find him on Instagram @JonathanReddochAuthor.

Michaela Rae

Michaela Rae is an emerging author with a background in English literature and multimedia design from the University of Utah. She began her storytelling journey at the *Salt Lake Tribune*, later transitioning to grant and marketing writing for nonprofits. She currently writes feminist dark fiction and poetry that explores power dynamics and resilience. Michaela lives in a historic Salt Lake City bungalow with her children, where she spends her time advocating for equity and capturing moments through photography.

Jennifer Leo

Jennifer Leo's passion for storytelling is rooted in her traditional Apache heritage. With a long-standing career as a professor of sociology and Native American studies, as well as a content developer, she has honed her skills in technical writing. She is now channeling her expertise into sci-fi/fantasy writing from an Indigenous perspective.

H.V. Patterson

H.V. Patterson writes speculative fiction and poetry from Oklahoma. Her work appears in *Etherea Magazine*, *Haven Speculative*, *hex literary*, *Wyldblood Press*, and anthologies from Flame Tree Press, Eerie River, and more. She's a co-founder of Horns and Rattles Press. Follow her on X @ScaryShelley and Instagram @hvpattersonwriter.

Natalya Monyok

Natalya Monyok is a horror writer specializing in transgressive and psychological subgenres. She's currently seeking representation for her novel *Mortal Minds* and is published in numerous horror anthologies. A Brazilian Jiu-Jitsu blue belt, she trains with the goal of becoming a world champion. She lives in Utah's rugged mountains with her dogs, Ares and Cain.

Steve Capone Jr.

Steve Capone Jr. is a multi-genre author nestled in Salt Lake County, Utah. A member of the Horror Writers Association and League of Utah Writers, Steve has received awards for both fiction and nonfiction. His work can be found in *We Are Dangerous* (2023) and *Inkpot Literary Journal* (2021). His debut YA historical novel *Jimmy vs. Communism* is set for release in early 2026. Favorite city: Berlin. Least favorite question: "What's your favorite color?"

Jordan McClymont

Jordan McClymont is a queer, working-class writer from Ayrshire, Scotland, now writing speculative fiction and screenplays. Their micro fiction has appeared in *365 Tomorrows* and *Ghostwatch Zine #23*. Jordan writes about poverty, identity, alienation, and the longing for community.

Eric J. Guignard

Eric J. Guignard is a Bram Stoker and Shirley Jackson Award-winning writer and anthologist of dark and speculative fiction. Based near Los Angeles, he has also been a finalist for the World Fantasy and International Thriller Writers Awards.

Ashley Huyge

Ashley Huyge is a writer, educator, and course designer whose work has appeared in *Darkness 101: Lessons Were Learned* and *Dreams Walking*. She is currently editing a speculative horror novel. Now living near Los Angeles, she enjoys shaded sunshine, movies, and coffee, alongside her husband, cats, and dreams.

F. Malanoche

F. Malanoche writes authentic and odd Latino stories under cover of night. An English teacher in the Midwest, he shares his life with a wonderful wife and a sweet vinyl collection. Find him on Facebook.

Puck Phillips

Puck Phillips, originally from Utah, writes fiction and haiku. In their spare time, they haunt indie bookstores and hike among the pines.

Robin Knabel

Robin Knabel is a horror author, the owner of Inky Bones Press, and a member of the HWA. Her stories can be found in numerous anthologies and online magazines. She enjoys drinking copious amounts of coffee & taking photographs. You can usually find her reading on her couch while being weighed down by a cat (or two). Learn more at www.robinknabel.com.

Tyler J. Welch

Tyler lives in Wisconsin with his wife and two sons. When not hiding from frigid winters, he explores forests and fog-shrouded marshes, drawing inspiration for his dark, atmospheric writing and photography. His debut novel, *End Realm*, releases in October 2024. Find more at tyler-jwelch.com and on Instagram @tylerjacksonwelch.

Jessica Gleason

Jessica Gleason is a Hawaiian-Italian author who pens horror and fantasy deep into the night. A college English and Communications professor by day, she paints monsters in acrylic and belts out hair metal karaoke. Her short novel *The Fabulous Miss Fortune* released in June 2023 from The Evil Cookie Publishing. Follow her on Instagram (@j.g.writes), where she hosts the monthly #WeWriteHorror challenge.

Kelli Dianne Rule

Kelli Dianne Rule is an artist and writer from rural west-central Florida. She delights in humor-laced dread and flawed protagonists. Her work appears in *Heavy Feather Review*, *101 Words*, *Creepy Podcast*, and forthcoming issues of *Whale Road Review*, *Blood Moon Rising*, and *Green Hills Literary Lantern*.

Morgana Price

Morgana Price (aka Alicia Morley Dodson) turns her eerie dreams into stories. Her pen name pays tribute to Morgana of Arthurian legend and horror icon Vincent Price. Featured in *Darkness 101* and *Collective Chaos*, Morgana is a gothic goddess at heart. She loves horror podcasts, floral photography, cupcakes, and being "mummy" to her son. Follow @morganapriceofficial.

K. R. Patterson

K. R. Patterson has believed in vampires, ghosts, and werewolves since childhood. Her horror has appeared in numerous *Darkness* anthologies, and her pirate novel *A Dead Man's Tale* is available on Amazon and Audible. A Writers Digest contributor and contest winner, she's pursuing an MFA and working on a novel about a cursed town.

Cailín Frankland

Cailín Frankland (she/they) is a British-American writer and public health professional living in Baltimore. Their work explores feminism, queerness, neurodivergence, and intergenerational trauma. Cailín shares life with their spouse, two elderly cats, and a pit bull named Baby.

Brianna Malotke

Brianna Malotke is a horror writer in the PNW with over 90 publications. A member of the HWA and co-chair of its Seattle chapter, she's been featured in *Under Her Skin*, *The Dire Circle*, and *HorrorScope*. Her debut poetry collection *Fashion Trends, Deadly Ends* came out in 2023, followed by *Lost Cherry* in 2024.

AudraKate Gonzalez

AudraKate Gonzalez wrote her first horror stories when she ran out of *Goosebumps* books. Now, with a BA in Creative Writing and an MFA in progress, she lives in Ohio with her husband and dogs, Zero and Scrappy Doo. When not writing, she reads, watches scary movies, or naps.

Hannah Grace

Hannah Grace infuses the macabre with vibrant imagination and feminist themes. She writes horror with strong female leads and finds creative fuel from her personal pack of "Hellhounds."

Sara Fitzgerald

Sara Fitzgerald is an award-winning, multi-published author and the 2006 League of Utah Writers' Writer of the Year. She won the 2024 Silver Quill in Novellas and lives in Salt Lake City with her husband and daughter. Halloween is one of her favorite holidays. sarafitzgeraldauthor.com

Charles Kyd

Charles Kyd remembers the night he first wrote a capital "A"—and he's been writing ever since. He may stop someday, but probably won't. Find him on LinkedIn.

Robert J. Foster

Robert J. Foster, author of *Morgan's Mount*, loves ghost stories, horror, crime fiction, and fantasy. A nature lover, you'll find him wandering the woods—or sipping coffee in a cozy café.

Thomas S. Salem

Thomas S. Salem holds a degree in English Literature and writes fiction and poetry. His work includes the short story "Solve for X" in *Darkness 101*, and poems "Tide Pool" and "Maternal" in *100Subtexts Magazine*.

Ethan Stewart

Ethan Stewart is a proud nerd who loves Dungeons & Dragons, video games, and reptiles. He lives with his dog, Marshmallow, and his snake, Yuji. Favorite reads: *Mistborn* and *Eragon*.

Jenny Castro

Jenny Castro, a storyteller with roots in El Salvador, blends multiculturalism into her narratives. A League of Utah Writers member, she draws inspiration from Pablo Neruda and the outdoors. She gardens with her schnauzers and enjoys national parks, always writing with authenticity and heart.

Ace Mack

Ace Mack's writing journey began with rap lyrics in his native Miami. Surrounded by vibrant cultures and causes, he draws from his diverse upbringing to craft stories that reflect the struggles, beauty, and truths of his community.

Andrew J. Pixton

Andrew Pixton is a writer and social worker whose passions—travel, martial arts, and philosophy—inspire his horror, dark fantasy, poetry, and soon-to-be science fiction. If he disappears, check the nearest mossy forest. He responds best to snacks with coconut or cinnamon.

Paul Lonardo

Paul Lonardo is a freelance writer and author of both fiction and nonfiction. He has contributed to numerous magazines and ezines and is a regular writer for *Tales from the Moonlit Path*. He is a proud member of the Horror Writers Association.

Keyra K. Allred

Keyra K. Allred is a lifelong reader and former Utah journalist. They've published short stories in magazines and online, and dream of traveling the world, writing, and spending time with animals—possibly with their husband tagging along. They live in the reluctant embrace of their two gingers, Richard and Eustace.

Devin Guignard

Devin Guignard is a new writer of horror short stories. This marks her first publication.

Mae Thorn

Mae Thorn loves being terrified and romanced—often simultaneously. She writes horror, fantasy, and historical romance, with three romance novels published: *Notorious*, *Dangerous*, and *Rebellious*. She holds degrees in English and Library Science. Mae co-presides over the League of Utah Writers Romance Chapter and lives near Salt Lake City with her cats Church, Shadow Moon, and Sabrina, and her pup, Whiskey.

Selene Lizeth Ibarra Rubio

Selene Lizeth Ibarra Rubio is an eighteen-year-old

Mexican writer and mechanical engineering student at San Jose State University. She writes across genres, especially horror, with a focus on humanity's relationship to nature and each other. This is her first publication.

J. B. Corso

J.B. Corso is a Midwest-based mental health clinician and horror writer. A parent and existential thinker, they write while listening to the Grateful Dead. A NaNoWriMo winner (2021–2023) and internationally published author, they have credits with Sirens Call Publications, Black Hare Press, The Dragon's Roost, and The Stygian Lepus.

Jayne Ann Osborne

Jayne Ann Osborne doesn't need horror—her overactive imagination supplies more than enough nightmares. Yet those nightmares inspire flash fiction. She's an artist, co-owner of Merry Robin Publishing, and author/illustrator of three children's books, including *When Mommies Get Sick*.

Elizabeth Rayne

Elizabeth Rayne is a creature who writes. Her work appears in *SYFY WIRE*, *Live Science*, *Den of Geek*, and *Forbidden Futures*, among others. Based near NYC, she lives with her parrot Lestat. When not writing, she draws, plays piano, or shapeshifts.

Alex Child

Alex Child knows writing's power—but not enough to describe it. When not overworking or underworking, he chases the feeling of connecting deeply with a fictional character. He hopes his stories offer even a piece of that emotional rush.

Gregory Meece

Gregory Meece is a retired educator turned storyteller, woodcarver, and Amish taxi driver. He holds multiple degrees and has been published in over twenty magazines and anthologies. He lives on a former Christmas tree farm in Pennsylvania. Learn more at meecetales.com.

Russell Evans

Russell Evans is a man both simple and complex.

Addison Hope

Addison Hope is a junior in high school who loves horror and writing from the antagonist's perspective. The youngest of four, she dreams of attending Washington State University and looks up to her older sisters.

Corinne Pollard

Corinne Pollard is a disabled indie horror/fantasy author in the UK. Her work appears with Black Hare Press, Inky Bones Press, and more. She holds a degree in English Lit and Creative Writing, and enjoys metal, graveyards, and book shopping. Follow her @CorinnePWriter.

Madison Parker

Madison Parker lives in Chattanooga, TN with her partner and two cats. A biology grad from the University of North Georgia, she works in insurance and writes horror and dark fantasy—usually in the company of animals, her preferred audience.

Amber Buckley

Amber Buckley has taught high school English and Creative Writing for over a decade. With a BA in Secondary Ed-ELA, she's passionate about literature and sarcasm. A mother of two, she prefers life behind the pages of a good book.

Debra Birdwell Winkler

Debra Birdwell Winkler is a former history teacher and published author of short stories, novels, and poems. Her debut novel released in November 2022, and she was nominated for the 2022 Best of the Net Nonfiction Award. A member of RWA and LUW Romance Chapter, she recommends reading her horror while listening to Rachmaninov's *Isle of the Dead*.

Peter L. Harmon

Peter L. Harmon spends his days wrangling a rambunctious pug and producing TV shows, screenplays, and a podcast. He also co-owns High Dive Publishing. His podcast *The VamPetey Diaries* is a *Vampire Diaries* rewatch show. Follow @HighDivePublishing and @ThePortableProducer on Instagram.

Joshua Booker

Joshua Booker is a sci-fi/fantasy/horror nerd who grew up in Milwaukee and became a wildlife biologist. He writes to process reality, channeling his love of ecology, justice, NBA basketball, and more. He lives in Ohio with his wife, kids, and many critters.

Anne Gregg

Anne Gregg is a college student, writer, and poet from Northwest Indiana. Her fiction appears in *Kids Are Hell!*, *Collective Fantasy*, and *Darkness 101*, and her poetry has been featured in *Noctivagant Press* and *The Black Poppy Review*.

Jo Birdwell

Jo Birdwell is a writer and nurse from Texas, working on a degree in English and Creative Writing. Her horror stories "The Mortician's Daughter" (*Deluxe Darkness*) and "Unlovable" (*Open Minds Quarterly*, 2022) reflect her deep love for the genre.

Makayla Nielson

Makayla Nielson, raised in Normal, Illinois, now lives in Lehi, Utah with her husband and three kids. She holds degrees in Family Studies and Gerontology and writes both fiction and academic pieces. Outside writing, she enjoys sci-fi movies, canyon hikes, and crochet—with snacks, always.

P.S. Tom

P.S. Tom is a husband, father, writer, and entrepreneur. When he's not building Halloween attractions for studios and musicians, he's writing horror and mystery short stories. He's also a real estate broker. Find him on Instagram @p.s.-tom_author.

M. L. Smythe

M.L. Smythe is a queer, non-binary author and nurse based in Florida's swamplands. They use fantasy and horror to process the trauma of healthcare work. They live in a beach town with their husband, two kids, and four cats.

Chris Jorgensen

Chris Jorgensen is a writer, musician, academic, scavenger, and horror enthusiast. He has written for UVU publications and is inspired by authors like Lovecraft, King, Abercrombie, and Sanderson. Horror allows him to explore the primal and unknown—and he's not done yet.